Don't miss the other stories in the
Lollapalooza short story series:

Quarantine
Common Enemies
Coiled Danger
Mars Meeting

R.W. WALLACE
AUTHOR OF THE VANGUARD

COILED DANGER

A LOLLAPALOOZA SHORT STORY

BOOK 3

Coiled Danger

by R.W. Wallace

Copyright © 2020 by R.W. Wallace

Copy editing by Jinxie Gervasio

Cover by the author

Cover Illustration 47588245 © algolonline | 123rf.com

All characters and events in this book, other than those clearly in the public domain, are fictitious and any resemblance to real persons, living or dead, is purely coincidental.

All rights reserved. No part of this publication may be reproduced, distributed, or transmitted in any form or by any means, including photocopying, recording, or other electronic or mechanical methods, without the prior written permission of the publisher, except in the case of brief quotations embodied in critical reviews and certain other noncommercial uses permitted by copyright law.

www.rwwallace.com

ISBN: [979-10-95707-39-4]

Main category—Fiction

Other category—Science Fiction

First Edition

Also by R.W. Wallace

Mystery

The Tolosa Mystery Series
The Red Brick Haze (free)
The Red Brick Cellars
The Red Brick Basilica

Ghost Detective Shorts (coming soon)
Just Desserts
Lost Friends
Family Bonds
Till Death
Common Ground

Short Stories
Hidden Horrors
Cold Blue Eternity
Critters
Gertrude and the Trojan Horse
First Impressions
Let Them Eat Cake
Two's Company

Science Fiction (short stories)
The Vanguard

Adventure (short stories)
Size Matters

Fantasy (short stories)
Morbier Impossible
A Second Chance
Unexpected Consequences

COILED DANGER

Anouk rolled her shoulders in an attempt to get rid of the ever-present itch between her shoulder blades and pulled a frustrated hand through her pink hair. Her fingers caught on a tangle and she winced at the pull on her scalp. She hadn't found the time for a shower today, which was completely unacceptable. Soon, she would start sporting pimples, and her colleagues would comment on the smell of unwashed body.

Anouk glanced over at the three guys working next to her. Okay, nobody would likely notice the odor.

What they *would* notice, was if the Lollapalooza's telecommunications system broke down. They'd already lost the Prime, and the Secondary circuit was showing signs of weakness. All calls going in and out suffered tiny interruptions—not enough to make it impossible to understand what anyone was saying, but enough to make Anouk's inner mechanic go on high alert.

They weren't living in the bloody Middle Ages, there shouldn't be *any* kind of issue in this part of the universe. On the outskirts of the known world, or on particularly primitive planets, sure. But they were in Earth's Solar System, for crying out loud. It didn't get any more central than that.

Anouk should have felt comfortable right now. She was surrounded by machines on all sides, humming along on the solar power she'd linked them up to just last week, beeps going off whenever a new communication was established, and tiny LED lights turning on or off depending on which part of the computer treated the current task.

This room housed the Secondary circuit and was usually in very little use. Anouk or one of the other mechanics would come here every three or four days to run a system check, but other than that, the room was usually quiet and empty.

Prime lived in an identical room at the other end of the ship. Where there used to be the noise of only machines, today it held a lot of human voices and clinking and clanking of tools.

Prime was where Anouk had spent the past three days. The first priority was to get the machine back up and running.

Until Captain Kovak asked why there were glitches on her radar and short interruptions in the communications channels.

At which point, Secondary became her first priority. If both Prime and Secondary went down, they were as good as dead. You can't travel safely through space if your automatic pilot doesn't know where it's going or what obstacles it might encounter on its way.

"Another one," Shorty said. Anouk really had to learn the guy's actual name instead of using Gaal's ridiculous nickname, but she'd already tried once and hadn't remembered it for more than the five seconds it took the guy to say it.

Shorty was, as his nickname implied, short. The captain and Gaal had apparently picked up him and his buddy—nickname: Shorter—on a planet where people were valued for their height. Shorty and Shorter had been at the very bottom of the food chain. Anouk supposed that was why they were both so short on initiative, but she had the hardest time finding adequate tasks for the both of them. With zero initiative, a mechanic—or anyone working on a space ship, really—is worthless.

He was able to watch for the glitches, though.

"How long was it?" Anouk asked.

"One and a half second," Shorty replied, never taking his eyes off the LED lights, determined not to miss the next one.

Anouk frowned. "You're sure? So it's longer than the last one?"

"Yes," Shorty confirmed. "By point two seconds."

"Interval since the last one?"

"Twenty-five minutes."

At least that hadn't changed. Every twenty-five minutes, they had a glitch. At the moment, it didn't represent a real danger, but if the glitches were getting longer…

"Keep a record of all glitches," she ordered Shorty. "Duration and frequency. If duration goes over two seconds or if the frequency changes, come get me. Wake me, if I'm sleeping."

Shorty glanced at her at this and his eyes seemed to widen—though it was difficult to say since they were so small to begin with. He wasn't keen on waking her up.

"I won't be mad if you wake me up as ordered," Anouk said. "But I'll skin you alive if you don't."

"Yes, sir." Shorty returned to his vigil.

☙

Anouk got two hours of sleep before Shorty woke her up by poking her in the arm.

"The last glitch was two seconds," he said.

Anouk bit back a growl as she opened her eyes. Two hours of sleep was *not* enough, but it was hardly Shorty's fault her beauty sleep was cut short. He was just following orders. Her orders.

"Thank you," she ground out. "Please keep watching and let me know if there are any changes. Tell me when we hit two and a half seconds," she specified when he hesitated. "Or if the frequency changes in any way."

Once the odd little man was out of her room, Anouk swung out of bed. She was already dressed—*still* dressed—since she'd had a feeling she wouldn't be getting much sleep and hadn't bothered with a shower or pajamas. She'd just lain down in her trusty fluorescent yellow tracksuit, accepting that until the problem with the Prime and the Secondary was solved, she was going to be a stinking mess.

Two minutes later she knocked on the captain's door.

"Come in," the captain's voice sounded. At least she wasn't asleep.

Anouk entered. The captain's bed looked like it hadn't been slept in since the last time the cleaning staff had been through here—more than fifteen hours ago. A novel occupied the bedside table, but Anouk could see the dust blanketing the jacket from her position at the door.

The office area looked like it saw much more use than the bed. Maps, tablets, and screens were spread out on all available surfaces, there were empty coffee cups all over the place, and there wasn't a speck of dust in sight.

Anouk expected to find Captain Kovak at her desk, but she hadn't expected her to have company. Yosu Gaal, the second-in-command, sat across from Kovak, three screens alight on the table between them. Lots of maps, plenty of annotations. And the man was chewing gum, like always.

"How's the repairs coming on the communications system?" the captain asked, her eyes on a map of the Earth's Solar System.

Gaal pretended to be looking at the maps, too, but Anouk guessed he'd be able to give more details on the beauty marks on the captain's face than on the moons of Saturn.

These two had been circling each other for weeks, but neither seemed to have the guts to actually take action.

"Prime's still down," Anouk reported. "Secondary's showing signs of weakness."

Both the captain's and Gaal's eyes snapped to meet Anouk's.

"What do you mean by sign of weakness?" Captain Kovak asked.

As Anouk explained, she could see the doubt in their eyes. Was their communications system really suffering from some mysterious weakness or wasn't she as good a mechanic as she'd advertised?

She hated not being able to find the source of their problem. She usually found a certain thrill in going after mysteries nobody else could solve, but she rarely had the safety of the entire ship depending on her figuring it out quickly. With everything being doubled or tripled, she could always rely on the backups while she took her time repairing whatever had broken down.

Now they were *already* on the backup.

The captain went straight to the heart of the problem. "What happens if one of these glitches occur when we're traveling through a wormhole?"

"I don't know," Anouk replied. "And I wouldn't want to test it."

Gaal looked down at the map in front of him, actually seeing it this time. "Most wormholes take over thirty minutes to navigate." He glanced at the captain before meeting Anouk's eyes again. "Does the phenomenon occur *every* twenty-five minutes?"

"It does."

The captain leaned back in her chair, frustration clear in her features. Her hair was its usual mess and the top two buttons of her shirt were open, but she still exuded confidence and competence. She let out a long breath. "You're saying we're stuck here at snail speed until you fix the thing?"

"Unless you want to risk all our lives, yes," Anouk replied with a wince.

"Will it help if I give you more manpower?"

Anouk shrugged. "A couple of men might help. But there's no point in sending me the entire crew."

The captain nodded and stood up. "You can have Gaal. And he'll find you a couple of more men." She tapped the screens to turn them off, one after the other. "I'm going to bed. When I wake up, please make sure we're ready for some real space travel?"

"Will do, Captain." Anouk saluted, then turned to Gaal with a grin. "Looks like I get to order you around for a change?"

Anouk should have gone back to sleep, but instead, she returned to Secondary. The glitches were getting longer and the captain didn't have faith in her—no way in hell would she get any sleep anytime soon.

She had six crew members working on finding the origin of the glitches. They were testing every single sub-system one by one, to make sure they were working correctly, logging activity, and checking the logs for the known times of every occurrence.

So far, they had nothing.

Everything was working correctly, except when a glitch appeared—then everything went offline for two seconds.

"Two point five seconds," Shorty reported.

Dammit.

"The source can't be just one instrument," Anouk said to Gaal, who so far, hadn't really done anything useful, only made her team nervous by looking over their shoulders while they worked. "If it was, it couldn't have affected the Prime all the way on the other side of the ship."

"If something broke down," Gaal said, "it could have happened the same way on both systems."

"It *could*. But the probability of it happening at the same time on both systems, after neither of them having had any issues over the past ten years, and Prime being in use about ten times as often as Secondary, is as close to nil as you can get." She spun around on herself as she took in the entire room, with its long walls covered in instruments, the low ceiling, the creaky linoleum floors. "The source has to be external."

Gaal lowered his voice so as not to be heard by the other crew members. "You think someone outside of our ship is messing with our communications systems?"

Anouk fought the urge to scratch the itch on her back. It had been getting worse ever since she boarded the Lollapalooza, making her jumpy. She eyed the ceiling again. "Not necessarily external to the ship. But external to the system, and this room, yes."

Gaal followed her gaze. "Want me to go get Shorty?"

☙

ANOUK HEAVED HERSELF into the dropped ceiling above the supply closet. If she'd read the blueprints correctly, the main ceiling was shared with the one from the Secondary room. She could have asked everybody to leave and just gone up from over there, but she wanted them to keep working—and she suddenly felt the need for secrecy.

If someone from their crew had tampered with the ship, she couldn't let them know she was onto them.

Which was why she'd turned down Gaal's offer to call on the crew's shortest member. Instead, the man himself pulled himself into the cramped space with her, his tall frame taking up all the light and space.

"Good thing I'm not claustrophobic," he said under his breath once he laid on his stomach next to Anouk, breathing heavily from the effort of fitting his entire body in there without putting weight on any of the parts that might fall down into the rooms below. Of course, if he hadn't insisted on chewing that damned gum all the time, he might have more opportunity to do things like breathing. From the smell of things, today's flavor was some sort of fruit.

"I'm sure you've been in worse situations," Anouk said absently as she flashed her light in the direction of the Secondary room. Some light filtered up through the cracks of the dropped ceiling, but if she wanted to find what she thought, she'd need real light. She started crawling forward.

"What are we looking for?" Gaal asked before stifling a cough. This place could need a clean-up.

"A coil." Anouk turned her head to listen to the space below them. She heard the voices of the men testing the Secondary's systems. She flashed her light along the dropped ceiling, but saw nothing but the metallic grid, the squares that formed the ceiling of the room below, and dust. It didn't look like anybody had been up here in months.

"A coil," Gaal repeated. "How big would that be? Thumbnail? Size of my hand?"

Everybody except Gaal and the captain were new on the Lollapalooza's crew. None of them had been on the ship for more than three weeks. Unless someone from the old crew was haunting them, she was not in the right place.

She flashed her light at the ceiling. "Size of the room," she finally answered Gaal. "If someone manages to create a coil around the entire room, then run enough power through it, it would create a magnetic field that would seriously impact the systems."

Gaal swore around his gum as he crawled along the dropped ceiling next to Anouk. "You're saying we're being deliberately messed with?"

"I'm saying I suspect it. It would explain the system's odd behavior."

Having crossed almost the entire space, they approached a wall. Judging by the men's voices below, they were still above the Secondary room. Anouk flashed her light along the ceiling.

Something reflected the light. At the next-to-last beam overhead, something was shinier than the rest of the beam.

"Over here," Anouk told Gaal and beckoned him over.

Several thin wires were attached to the beam—duct tape, by the looks of it—running from one end of the room to the other. At one end, it turned downward and disappeared through the dropped ceiling, at the other, it continued through a hole in the wall.

Whoever had done this must have come up using a different route. This area was clean of dust, all along the space below the beam, as if someone had crawled passed there quite recently.

Gaal touched a finger to the wires. "How powerful a magnetic field can this create?" he whispered.

"Right now," Anouk answered, "enough to give us two and a half second glitches."

"The glitches have been getting longer." His eyes met hers, the light from the moving flashlight making his jaw look even more angular than usual.

Anouk scratched a nail over the remains of removed duct tape. "Every time they add a wire, it gets a little stronger."

Gaal's head snapped around as if expecting someone to pop out of the dropped ceiling any minute. There was nobody there, of course, so his attention returned to Anouk. "Why not add everything at once?"

Anouk tried to picture the blueprints she saw earlier to figure out where the wires might be going to get around the entire Secondary room. There must be some sort of placard or ventilation chute. If the wires went through the hallway that everybody walked through every day, someone would have noticed.

She answered Gaal's question. "You can't just add wires around, willy-nilly. It has to be one really long wire going round and round. You send electricity through, and you get a magnetic field. This"—she pointed to the wires—"is a work in progress."

Anouk reached into her utility belt—yellow to go with her track suit because that was just how she rolled—to retrieve her pliers. "Luckily, it doesn't take much to ruin their effort."

"Wait." Gaal reached out a hand to stop her before she could cut the offending wires. "If you cut that, the next time they send power through, it's not going to create the glitch, right?"

"Yes. That's why I'm going to cut them."

"As long as we don't venture into any wormholes, do the glitches really represent a danger to the ship?"

Anouk ground her teeth. Her fingers itched to get rid of the stuff interfering with her machines. "There's a slight increase in our risk of hitting an asteroid or space trash, but no, not really."

Gaal pulled Anouk's hand away from the wires. "Then we're going to leave it. And put this place under surveillance." He chewed on his gum like it was personally responsible for putting his ship and crew in danger. "I want to know who did this, and I want to know why."

ଓ

They set up the surveillance in the restrooms. After following the wires, they discovered the stack of wire yet to be set up in the dropped ceiling over the sinks. Whoever set this up was seriously motivated, because it must be quite the job to pull the wire through dropped ceilings, through walls, through the space below the floors… They found the power source: the wire was linked to the solar panels Anouk had recently installed—and didn't that hurt. What she'd worked hard to set up was being used against her.

While Gaal stood watch, Anouk went into the dropped ceiling over Prime. She knew what to expect, but it was still a shock to see the wires covering an entire overhead beam. She measured the strength of the magnetic field and had to restrain herself from cutting the wires when she saw the reading.

It was a miracle this thing hadn't crashed the entire ship.

Here, they'd tapped into the main generator and hadn't bothered with limiting what they took in order to minimize the risk of detection. The pulses flew through the wires every thirty seconds, effectively stopping Prime from as much as starting up.

"Roux," Gaal's voice came through the intercom in Anouk's ear. "I think our bad guy is here. Come back—"

He was cut off. No amount of tapping her ear bud brought Gaal's voice back.

Anouk sped across the ship while calling the captain on a secure line.

"Gaal might be in trouble in the bathroom next to Secondary," she huffed out between breaths. "I lost contact with him less than a minute ago."

Captain Kovak's voice was rough from sleep. "I'm on my way."

Three minutes later, Anouk sprinted into the bathroom, a wrench she'd picked up on the way ready in her right hand, in case someone needed their head banged in.

She was met with what appeared to be an octopus on the bathroom floor. A large, black mass was writhing on the white tiles, arms and legs flailing—

Anouk caught her breath and her eyes agreed to work on putting things into focus again. She really should consider getting glasses.

Gaal had somebody pinned to the floor, but whoever it was, wasn't giving up, which made the both of them turn around in circles as one wanted to free arms and legs, and the other followed and pinned down every single moving limb.

Gaal had some fighting skills. Then again, he was a trained police officer.

Something crunched under Anouk's foot—Gaal's ear bud. "Sorry," she said, though Gaal wasn't exactly paying attention.

"Grab an arm, will you?" Gaal panted as he pinned down one leg, only to have an arm break free.

Anouk leaned the wrench against the wall next to the door. "Sure thing." Waiting for the next time an arm came within striking distance, she lashed out and grabbed an arm that was almost free from Gaal's grasp.

It was all Gaal needed to obtain the upper hand in the fight. With Anouk still holding onto one limb, he managed to subdue the rest of his opponent, ending up kneeling on the other guy's back and neck with one arm twisted backward.

"Thank you, Roux," Gaal said, as if she'd brought him a cup of coffee. "You can let go now."

Anouk got one good look at the guy below Gaal and went back to retrieve her wrench. "That's Gerard," she stated stupidly. A guy from Earth who'd come onboard the Lollapalooza at the same time as Anouk. He was built like a truck and was worth his weight in gold for cooking the best meals Anouk had ever had aboard a ship.

Too many questions vied for attention in Anouk's mind, and the least important one slipped out. "How did he even manage to get into the dropped ceiling?"

Gaal gave her an odd look, which turned into a relieved smile when the captain came through the door. "I'll make sure to ask him, just as soon as we have him secured in the holding cell."

଼

ONCE GERARD REALIZED he was well and truly caught, he stopped fighting. He went along meekly to the holding cell, where he sat calmly waiting until he was transported to an interrogation room.

The Lollapalooza didn't actually *have* an interrogation room, but the infirmary on the top floor had a sturdy lock and means of surveillance, so they made do.

As Anouk took her seat behind Captain Kovak and Gaal, she breathed a relieved sigh. She'd been allowed to remove the wires from both Prime and Secondary and she imagined this was what European ladies in the good old days felt like when they removed their corset after a long day—she could finally breathe again.

Her machines were doing fine. Secondary was still running things until they'd made extensive checks of Prime to make sure there was no lasting damage, but Prime should be up and running smoothly within a day or two.

She could have left the interrogation for the captain and her sidekick, but Gerard had messed with her machines. Anouk needed to know why and she needed to make sure the man would never come in contact with vital machinery ever again.

"Why did you take out our communications systems?" Captain Kovak asked Gerard. She sat in the nurse's chair, with Gaal next to her and the table separating them from the giant of a man. Judging from the captain's tone, she took the crime as seriously as Anouk, making her rise even further in Anouk's esteem.

Gerard shrugged.

"You just felt like it?" the captain asked. "Figured it would be fun to fly through space with nothing to guide us?"

Gerard stayed silent.

"What would you have done if we'd attempted to go through a wormhole? Was this a suicide mission?"

Gerard's gaze wandered to the right edge of the desk and a muscle ticked in his jaw.

The captain marked a pause, showing she wasn't bothered in the least by the silence.

"We found the survival 'chute in your bunk," the captain finally said. "You were going to eject just before we went into the next wormhole, huh?"

Gerard's eyes jumped to meet the captain's. Busted.

With a glance, the captain turned the interrogation over to Gaal.

"All right," Gaal said, blowing a bubble with his gum. He usually just chewed the stuff. Anouk didn't know him well enough to determine if a bubble meant he was at ease or stressed out. "So we know you were here to get us killed. The question is why. The good thing here is, there aren't that many possible motivations since up until the moment I hired you, there were only four persons on this ship. And two of them are sitting here across from you."

He chewed his gum as he studied Gerard. "I guess it's possible you're after Shorty and Shorter, but it doesn't seem likely. I didn't find any link between you and that weird-ass planet of theirs." He leaned forward, bracing his elbows on the desk. "So you're either after me, or the captain."

It seemed more likely he was after Gaal. As far as Anouk knew, the captain hadn't—

Gerard's eyes flicked to Anouk.

Anouk's breath caught. She'd had a rather intense conversation with Gaal a few weeks ago, talking about their pasts and possible grudges for wrongs done them and the people they loved.

They'd been in the mess hall, with only a door separating them from the kitchen—and Gerard.

"Gaal," Anouk said, her voice wavering because her pulse was going through the roof. "Did you recruit Gerard before or after you recruited me?"

Gaal turned to look at Anouk, an annoyed frown marring his forehead. However, when he saw her expression, the frown deepened into worry. "He was the last one to come aboard."

Anouk swallowed. She wanted to remind Gaal about their conversation but couldn't bring herself to mention it in front of the captain. She *had* pushed him to take action and get revenge for what happened to his crew on the day her father died, which might not be quite in line with what the captain had planned for them.

Gaal didn't need the reminder. His eyes widened in realization and he stopped chewing.

He shifted his gaze to the captain, actually removed his gum and slipped it into a tissue before talking, his voice rougher than usual. "He's after Roux and myself, Captain. I *will* explain everything, but I'd really appreciate it if we could avoid doing it in front of Gerard."

The captain's eyes narrowed. Her lips twitched down once.

Anouk held back a sigh. This wasn't going to help them resolve their attraction.

"I'll hold you to that, Yosu," Captain Kovak said. She gestured to their prisoner. "I'll let you lead for now. Since you clearly have information I don't."

Gaal's eyes lingered on the captain for several moments. The resignation in his eyes made for yet another point to add to the list of grievances against Gerard.

Straightening his back and taking a deep breath, Gaal turned to Gerard. "Were you after me or Roux?"

Gerard just stared back, his sullen eyes making Anouk think of a teenager having had quite enough of his parents' yapping but knowing he wouldn't get out of it anytime soon.

"Who do you work for? The pirates? The police?"

The captain's hands twitched in her lap, but Anouk was the only one to see it since she was sitting behind her.

"Do I really have to start making threats?" Gaal's face had gone hard, a look Anouk had never seen on him before. Suddenly, she could see him as the commander of a police vessel, with the respect of an entire team.

He folded his hands on the desk. "Shall we start by your source of income? You've been a chef for fifteen years, moving from ship to ship every eighteen months or so. Now, you *could* be like Roux here, and want to change to get new challenges and new things to do, but I don't buy it. Every time you changed employers, your salary went up considerably.

"Now, we all like having more money, don't we? But we don't all have three families depending on us back home."

Gerard had kept a stony expression and his eyes locked on a spot on Gaal's chin since the beginning of the questioning, but at this he actually looked the other man in the eyes. His face didn't change an iota, but a bead of sweat appeared on his temple.

"Your brother and two sisters just keep popping out new kids, don't they?" Gaal continued. "Figuring you'll find a way to send them more money. It's what you've always done, after all. But there *are* limits to what you can make as a chef, and I believe you met that limit a couple of jobs ago. And yet…you accepted to work for us for *less* than what you made on your last missions."

Gaal chewed on thin air, realized he didn't have his gum, and flexed his jaw instead. "I'm not an unreasonable man, Gerard. Nor is the captain. I'm thinking we can come to an understanding. After all, you still need to feed all those mouths, don't you?"

Gerard stayed immobile for several moments, before finally giving a curt nod.

"Here's what I can offer you," Gaal said. "And there's no point in negotiating, because it's all you're going to get." He held up one finger. "You jump ship with your 'chute when we're done here. I'll even leave you a radio so you can call for help." A second finger. "We won't tell anyone what you did, so long as you don't mention to anyone what happened here and what you heard. If you do, I'll know, and make sure you'll never find work anywhere ever again. Understood?"

This time the nod was immediate. The bead of sweat had worked its way down Gerard's chin, but a gleam of hope lit up his eyes.

Gaal held up a third finger. "In return, you tell us everything. Which one of us you're tailing and trying to kill. Everything you know about the reason why. Who you're working for. Everything. I find out you've left something out—bye bye career." He chewed on air again and with a frustrated growl, pulled a pink packet out of his pocket and popped a piece of gum into his mouth. "Do we have a deal, Gerard?"

Gerard nodded.

ღ

ANOUK BIT HER lip to keep from interrupting Gaal. He was her superior officer and called the shots, not to mention her best chance at ever finding out who was responsible for killing her father.

But he was going to let Gerard go.

The man had tried to get them all killed. He cooked for them every day, all the while planning a way for them to disappear through a wormhole to never find their way out. He'd been their friend, then stabbed them in the back.

He'd messed with her *machines*.

And he would get away without a scratch? Anouk opened her mouth to say something, anything.

Gerard started talking.

※

He'd been on the watch for the both of them. Anouk Roux and Yosu Gaal. That was his complete watch list.

If either one was spotted, he was to report on it.

If he had the possibility of getting close to either, he was to do it.

If either showed any signs of searching for the people responsible for that fateful day years ago, when Anouk's father and Gaal's team died, he was to report immediately and stop them, if necessary.

If they teamed up, he was to kill them as soon as possible, without trace, if at all possible.

The bonus he'd get for that last one was enough to make three sets of jaws drop to the floor.

He'd eavesdropped on Gaal and Anouk's conversation in the mess hall, of course. He'd reported the incident and started on his plan to make the whole ship disappear.

Gaal stayed immobile during the confession, but he was breathing heavily. "Who do you report to?" he asked when Gerard stopped talking.

"I just have a number I send everything to. In theory, there could be a response, but I've never had one. I don't know who's on the other end."

"How much have you reported recently?"

Gerard studied his nails. "They know the Prime is down. That I estimated two or three days to be able to do the same to Secondary. That you two have decided to go after them."

The captain's hands twitched again, but she said nothing. Gaal was going to have some explaining to do once this was over.

"I'm going to keep your phone," Gaal said. "Does it have the history of what you've sent them so far? So I can see the way you usually format your messages?"

Gerard nodded.

"What about money?" the captain asked. "Where does that come from?"

Gerard gave a defeated shrug. "From some bank account. Just a number. I'll give it to you."

Gaal and the captain shared a glance that Anouk couldn't read. It was like hanging out with a married couple.

Captain Kovak stood. "That'll be all for now, Gerard. You'll stay here until further notice."

Gerard bowed his head. "Yes, Captain."

෮ඨ

Someone was watching her. Some guy out there with enough money to pay an army of spies to look for her watched her every move, checked who she talked to and what she talked about.

Ever since her father's death, Anouk had felt an itch between her shoulder blades as if someone was watching her. She'd written it off as grief or paranoia—something she'd had to deal with her entire childhood while growing up on a pirate spaceship—and found ways to deal with it.

The pink hair. The purple eyebrows. The flashy clothes. All to attract people's attention and thereby explaining and drowning out the itch.

Mostly, it worked.

She'd had one talk with Gaal, and it changed everything. Gaal came to several realizations, looking at the information he already had from a different angle, seeing he wasn't guilty of killing his entire crew.

Anouk learned the hit on her father had been premeditated. It wasn't luck that brought Gaal's team to that part of the universe that day. Two of her father's crew ratted him out. And someone set it up so the police and the pirates would blow each other up instead of proceeding with a peaceful arrest.

Whoever it was also paid Gerard a lot of money to keep tabs on them, and then kill them when they came too close to the truth.

Whoever it was had to pay.

And she wanted that truth.

Anouk stood in the now empty Secondary room, her hands on the silent screens on the wall. Secondary had done its work and kept the ship on course while its twin Prime was down. Now Prime was up and running, bringing Secondary back to its role of back-up. Back to sleep.

Anouk wasn't going back to sleep, though.

She'd let Gaal deal with the captain and whatever backlash that would bring. Then they were tracking down those phone and account numbers.

She was getting rid of that itch.

AUTHOR'S NOTE

THANK YOU FOR reading *Coiled Danger*. I hope you enjoyed the story.

If you liked the story, you might want to check out the other stories of the Lollapalooza short story series. The adventure continues as Yosu, Anouk, and the captain try to figure out what happened the day Yosu lost his team and Anouk her father.

I also write in a bunch of other genres. You can, for example, pick up the first book in my Tolosa Mystery series for free on my website.

R.W. Wallace
www.rwwallace.com

Also by R.W. Wallace

Mystery

The Tolosa Mystery Series
The Red Brick Haze (free)
The Red Brick Cellars
The Red Brick Basilica

Ghost Detective Shorts (coming soon)

Just Desserts
Lost Friends
Family Bonds
Till Death
Family History
Common Ground
Heritage
Eternal Bond
New Beginnings

Short Stories
Cold Blue Eternity
Hidden Horrors
Critters
Gertrude and the Trojan Horse
First Impressions
Let Them Eat Cake
Out of Sight
Two's Company
Like Mother Like Daughter

Fantasy (Short Stories)
Unexpected Consequences
Morbier Impossible
A Second Chance

Science Fiction (Short Stories)
The Vanguard

Lollapalooza Shorts
Quarantine
Common Enemies
Coiled Danger
Mars Meeting

Adventure (Short Stories)
Size Matters

ABOUT THE AUTHOR

R.W. WALLACE WRITES in most genres, though she tends to end up in mystery more often than not. Dead bodies keep popping up all over the place whenever she sits down in front of her keyboard.

The stories mostly take place in Norway or France; the country she was born in and the one that has been her home for two decades. Don't ask her why she writes in English – she won't have a sensible answer for you.

Her Ghost Detective short story series appears in *Pulphouse Magazine*, starting in issue #9.

www.rwwallace.com

www.ingramcontent.com/pod-product-compliance
Lightning Source LLC
LaVergne TN
LVHW041717060526
838201LV00043B/778